Team Spirit

THE OAKLAND A's

BY

MARK STEWART

Content Consultant
James L. Gates, Jr.
Library Director
National Baseball Hall of Fame and Museum

NORWOOD HOUSE PRESS

CHICAGO, ILLINOIS

Norwood House Press
P.O. Box 316598
Chicago, Illinois 60631

For information regarding Norwood House Press, please visit our website at:
www.norwoodhousepress.com or call 866-565-2900.

All photos courtesy of Getty Images except the following:
Sweet Caporal (6); SSPC (7); Black Book archives (9, 23, 35 top left & bottom right, 41 bottom);
Topps, Inc. (14, 22, 35 bottom left, 36, 38, 41 top, 43); Williams Baking (16);
Goudey Gum Co. (17, 21, 40 top); Ramly (20);
Author's collection (31, 34 bottom left & right, 37).
Cover photo by Michael Zagaris/Getty Images.
Special thanks to Topps, Inc.

Editor: Mike Kennedy
Designer: Ron Jaffe
Project Management: Black Book Partners, LLC.
Special thanks to David Ulate.

Library of Congress Cataloging-in-Publication Data

Stewart, Mark, 1960-
   The Oakland A's / by Mark Stewart ; content consultant, James L. Gates, Jr.
       p. cm. -- (Team spirit)
   Summary: "Presents the history, accomplishments and key personalities of the Oakland Athletics baseball team. Includes timelines, quotes, maps, glossary and websites"--Provided by publisher.
   Includes bibliographical references and index.
   ISBN-13: 978-1-59953-170-0 (library edition : alk. paper)
   ISBN-10: 1-59953-170-4 (library edition : alk. paper) 1. Oakland Athletics (Baseball team)--History--Juvenile literature. I. Gates, James L. II. Title.
GV875.O24S84 2008
796.357'640979466--dc22
                                                    2007043504

COVER PHOTO: The A's get ready to greet a teammate after a thrilling win in 2007.

Table of Contents

SPORTS WORDS & VOCABULARY WORDS: In this book, you will find many words that are new to you. You may also see familiar words used in new ways. The glossary on page 46 gives the meanings of baseball words, as well as "everyday" words that have special baseball meanings. These words appear in **bold type** throughout the book. The glossary on page 47 gives the meanings of vocabulary words that are not related to baseball. They appear in ***bold italic type*** throughout the book.

Meet the A's

The Bay Area of Northern California is one of the most *diverse* and *dynamic* parts of the United States. It is home to San Francisco—one of America's best known cities—and Silicon Valley, the nickname for the area where many computer companies are located. The hardworking city of Oakland sits on the northern side of the bay. It may be less famous than its neighbors, but it is just as proud.

Oakland has a lot of pride in its sports teams, including the Athletics, or A's. The A's are not afraid to do things a little differently than other teams. Over the years, they have had different uniforms, different hairstyles, and different *strategies*. Oakland also takes the field with a whole different attitude, which is what the fans love most about the team.

This book tells the story of the A's. They are a team of new ideas, but they are not a new team. In fact, their roots stretch back more than 100 years and 3,000 miles. They have had some of the best teams and greatest players ever to step onto a baseball diamond.

The A's congratulate each other after a victory during the 2007 season.

Way Back When

Go West, young man. That was a popular saying in the 1800s in the United States. The West was filled with great promise and opportunity. The A's followed this advice—though Oakland is actually the team's third home. The club began in 1901 as the Philadelphia Athletics. Though the team is still officially known as the Athletics, fans have been calling them the A's as long as anyone can remember.

The early A's teams in Philadelphia were among the best in the **American League (AL)**. They were managed for 50 years by Connie Mack, who built a winning foundation on pitching, defense, and base-stealing. Mack's first group of stars included Harry Davis, Frank Baker, Eddie Collins, Eddie Plank, Charles "Chief" Bender, and Rube Waddell. All are in the **Hall of Fame**, except for Davis.

During the 1920s, Mack rebuilt the A's as a power-hitting team. **Sluggers** such as Al Simmons and Jimmie Foxx competed with Babe Ruth and Lou Gehrig of the New York Yankees for the home run and

runs batted in (RBI) championships. Mickey Cochrane and Lefty Grove made up the best catcher-pitcher combination in baseball. Philadelphia won the **pennant** each year from 1929 to 1931. Grove was the first winner of the AL **Most Valuable Player (MVP)** Award, also in 1931.

The A's struggled for the rest of their time in Philadelphia. They had a few stars, including Bob Johnson, Wally Moses, Ferris Fain, Gus Zernial, and Bobby Shantz. However, they were rarely in a pennant race later than June.

After Mack retired, the A's moved to Kansas City, Missouri. They played there from 1955 to 1967, but never had a winning season. In 1968, the A's moved farther west to Oakland. Many of the young players signed in Kansas City became stars in their new home city. Catfish Hunter, Blue Moon Odom, Vida Blue, and Rollie Fingers helped the A's form the best **pitching staff** in the league. Reggie Jackson, Sal Bando, and Joe Rudi were the heart of a powerful offense.

LEFT: A souvenir pin featuring Eddie Collins.
ABOVE: Rollie Fingers, one of the leaders of the A's in the 1970s.

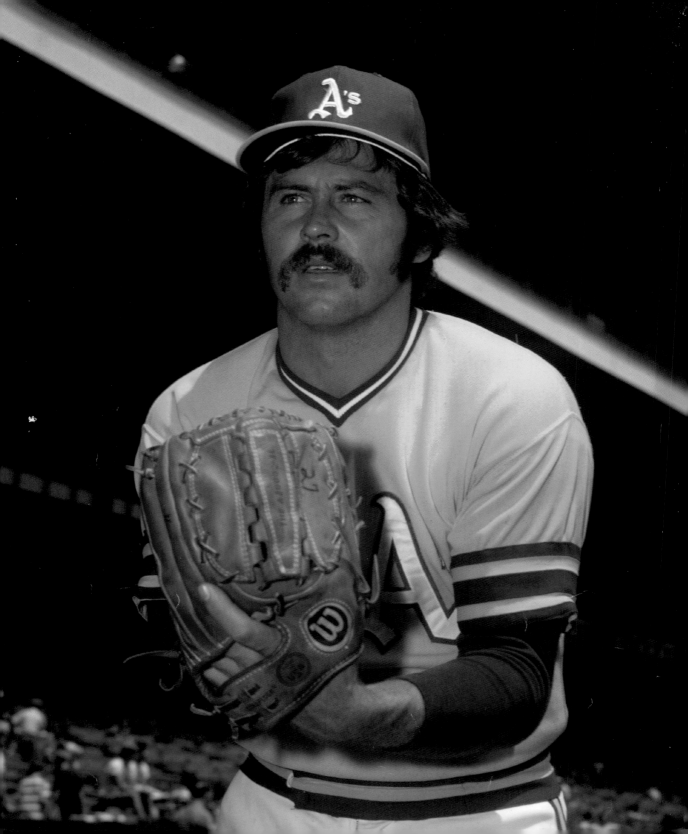

The A's won three **World Series** in a row from 1972 to 1974. They were known as the "Moustache Gang" because the team's owner, Charles Finley, paid his players a bonus to grow moustaches. The team wore stunning green and gold uniforms.

During the 1980s and 1990s, the A's kept playing exciting baseball. Rickey Henderson, Carney Lansford, Jose Canseco, and Mark McGwire were among the best hitters in baseball. Pitchers Dave Stewart and Dennis Eckersley were at their best in big games. Oakland won three more pennants from 1988 to 1990.

As the 21st *century* began, the A's were still finding new ways to win. This time the focus was on starting pitching and *patient* hitting. If Oakland's batters did not see good pitches, they simply refused to swing. This strategy gave the A's a lot of baserunners, a lot of runs, and a lot of victories. In no time, they had found the key to becoming a great team again.

LEFT: Jim "Catfish" Hunter, Oakland's best pitcher during the 1970s.
ABOVE: Rickey Henderson and Jose Canseco, two of the stars who led the A's back to the top of baseball.

The Team Today

The A's made it to the **playoffs** each year from 2000 to 2003. They got there on the strong arms of Barry Zito, Tim Hudson, and Mark Mulder. Thanks to those three pitchers, the A's always had a chance to win. The team also featured strong hitters, including Jason Giambi, Miguel Tejada, and Eric Chavez.

Unfortunately, that group of players fell short of another championship. Over time, many of those stars joined other teams. They were replaced by younger players such as Dan Haren, Joe Blanton, Nick Swisher, and Huston Street, the 2005 AL **Rookie of the Year**. That group combined great talent on the field with fun personalities off it.

Today's A's are focused on rewarding their fans with another trip to the World Series. As always, they look to the victories of the team's past to guide them. That means playing the game with skill and intelligence—and never being afraid to try something new.

Nick Swisher and Joe Blanton pose for the camera during the 2007 season.

Home Turf

When the Athletics played in Philadelphia, their home for most of those years was Shibe Park. It was later renamed Connie Mack Stadium in honor of the team's beloved manager. The A's played in Municipal Stadium after they moved to Kansas City. It was famous for its petting zoo, which was the home of the team's *mascot*, a mule named Charlie-O.

The A's moved into the Oakland-Alameda County Coliseum when they arrived in California in 1968. Pitchers love the field because it has a lot of room in foul territory for catching pop-ups. Hitters dislike it for the same reason. The stadium was originally built for the Oakland Raiders football team, but it is a great place to watch baseball, too. Since 2004, the stadium has been known as McAfee Coliseum.

BY THE NUMBERS

- *The team's stadium has 48,219 seats for baseball.*
- *The distance from home plate to the left field foul pole is 330 feet.*
- *The distance from home plate to the center field fence is 400 feet.*
- *The distance from home plate to the right field foul pole is 330 feet.*

This view of Oakland's stadium shows the large amount of space in foul territory down the right field line.

Dressed for Success

During their years in Philadelphia, the A's used blue and white as their team colors. In most years, the players wore a big letter *A* on their jerseys. Starting in 1929, their caps featured an *A*, too. The team was best known for its elephant **logo** in those days. After the A's moved to Kansas City, their full name (*Athletics*) was spelled out on their uniform for the first time. Later, the letters *KC* replaced the *A* on the team's cap.

In the 1960s, the A's began wearing sleeveless tops. They also changed their team colors to green and gold and started using a capital *A* on their uniforms again.

For many years, the A's were the most colorful team in baseball. For some road games, they wore gold pants and tops. In 1972, the A's switched to traditional uniform tops again. In 1988, the elephant reappeared on their sleeves. The A's have experimented with different uniform styles and logos since then, but green remains the team's main color.

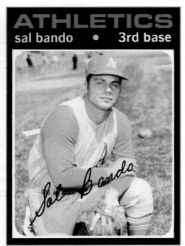

Sal Bando models the team's sleeveless uniform top and colorful green and gold look.

UNIFORM BASICS

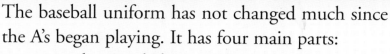

The baseball uniform has not changed much since the A's began playing. It has four main parts:

- a cap or batting helmet with a sun visor
- a top with a player's number on the back
- pants that reach down between the ankle and the knee
- stirrup-style socks

The uniform top sometimes has a player's name on the back. The team's name, city, or logo is usually on the front. Baseball teams wear light-colored uniforms when they play at home and darker styles when they play on the road.

For more than 100 years, baseball uniforms were made of wool *flannel* and were very baggy. This helped the sweat *evaporate* and gave players the freedom to move around. Today's uniforms are made of *synthetic* fabrics that stretch with players and keep them dry and cool.

Bobby Crosby takes a swing in one of Oakland's 2007 home uniforms.

We Won!

MACK, Mgr., ATHLETICS

The A's won nine World Series in a span of 80 years, the first in 1910 and the last in 1989. The first championship team featured base-stealer Eddie Collins and pitcher Jack Coombs. The A's faced the Chicago Cubs in the World Series and defeated them easily. Coombs won three times.

The A's won the World Series again in 1911. This time, they defeated the New York Giants four games to two. The hero for the A's was their hard-hitting third baseman, Frank Baker. He slammed *dramatic* home runs off New York's best pitchers to help the A's win two close games. Philadelphia beat the Giants again in the 1913 World Series. Baker and Chief Bender led the A's to victory, this time in five games.

The A's might have kept winning were it not for a new league called the **Federal League**. Many of the team's best players were offered more money to join the "Feds." Connie Mack could not afford to match those offers. It took 15 years before he was able to build another great team.

From 1929 to 1931, the A's ruled the AL. They beat the Cubs in the 1929 World Series and the St. Louis Cardinals in 1930. The Cardinals defeated the A's in 1931. Lefty Grove, Jimmie Foxx, Mickey Cochrane, and Al Simmons were the team leaders in those years. However, it was the great play of lesser-known A's such as Bing Miller, Howard Ehmke, and George Earnshaw that turned Philadelphia into a champion.

After moving to Oakland, the A's won three World Series in a row from 1972 to 1974. Those teams had great pitching, including Catfish Hunter, Vida Blue, Ken Holtzman, and Rollie Fingers. They also had good hitters, including Bert Campaneris, Sal Bando, Joe Rudi, and Reggie Jackson.

LEFT: Connie Mack, who managed the A's to five championships.
ABOVE: Jimmie Foxx, Al Simmons, and Mickey Cochrane formed the heart of Mack's batting order in the 1920s and 1930s.

Jackson was injured and did not play in the 1972 World Series against the Cincinnati Reds. But Hunter beat the Reds twice, and a little-used catcher named Gene Tenace supplied all the power Oakland needed to win in seven games. Jackson was in good shape for the 1973 World Series against the New York Mets. He got the winning hits in Game Six and Game Seven. Fingers was the star in 1974 against the Los Angeles Dodgers— the first ever "all-California" World Series.

The A's won three pennants in a row again from 1988 to 1990. Jose Canseco, Mark McGwire, Rickey Henderson, and Carney Lansford powered the Oakland offense. Dave Stewart, Bob Welch, and Dennis Eckersley were the team's top pitchers.

The A's were defeated in the World Series in 1988 and 1990, but in 1989 they swept the San Francisco Giants. The four games took 14 days to play because of a deadly earthquake in the Bay Area. Stewart and Henderson were the leading players for the A's. The Oakland victory was an impressive one—the team did not trail the Giants for a single inning.

ABOVE: Reggie Jackson takes a mighty swing during the 1973 World Series.   **RIGHT**: The A's celebrate their championship in 1989.

Go-To Guys

To be a true star in baseball, you need more than a quick bat and a strong arm. You have to be a "go-to guy"—someone the manager wants on the pitcher's mound or in the batter's box when it matters most. Fans of the A's have had a lot to cheer about over the years, including these great stars …

THE PIONEERS

EDDIE PLANK   Pitcher

• BORN: 8/31/1875 • DIED: 2/24/1926 • PLAYED FOR TEAM: 1901 TO 1914

Eddie Plank stepped toward first base when he pitched, then threw the ball across his body toward home plate. This "cross-fire" style confused most hitters. Plank won 20 or more games for the A's seven times.

PLANK
Pitcher, Athletics A. L.

EDDIE COLLINS   Second Baseman

• BORN: 5/2/1887 • DIED: 3/25/1951
• PLAYED FOR TEAM: 1906 TO 1914 & 1927 TO 1930

Eddie Collins was one of the smartest and fastest players in baseball. Collins helped the A's win six pennants. He led the league in runs scored each year from 1912 to 1914.

ABOVE: Eddie Plank   **RIGHT**: Al Simmons

20

AL SIMMONS   Outfielder

- Born: 5/22/1902 • Died: 5/26/1956
- Played for Team: 1924 to 1932, 1940 to 1941 & 1944

No one played harder than Al Simmons. He was a powerful hitter, good fielder, and an excellent baserunner. The right-handed Simmons used an extra-long bat because he stepped toward third base when he swung.

MICKEY COCHRANE   Catcher

- Born: 4/6/1903 • Died: 6/28/1962
- Played for Team: 1925 to 1933

Catchers were not expected to be great hitters when Mickey Cochrane played. He made fans look at his position in a different way. From 1929 to 1931, Cochrane batted better than .340, and the A's won the pennant each year.

LEFTY GROVE   Pitcher

- Born: 3/6/1900 • Died: 5/22/1975 • Played for Team: 1925 to 1933

Many experts believe that Lefty Grove was baseball's best pitcher during his years with the A's. He led the AL in strikeouts in each of his first seven seasons and had the lowest **earned run average (ERA)** in the league four years in a row.

JIMMIE FOXX   First Baseman

- Born: 10/22/1907 • Died: 7/21/1967 • Played for Team: 1925 to 1935

Jimmie Foxx was one of the strongest sluggers in history. He once shattered a seat in the upper deck of Yankee Stadium. Another time, he hit a ball over the roof of Chicago's Comiskey Park. Foxx slammed 58 home runs in 1932 and won the **Triple Crown** in 1933.

MODERN STARS

CATFISH HUNTER　　　　　　　　　　　　　Pitcher

- BORN: 4/8/1946　　• DIED: 9/9/1999　　• PLAYED FOR TEAM: 1965 TO 1974

The A's had many good pitchers in the 1970s, but Jim "Catfish" Hunter was the best. He won 20 or more games four years in a row. Hunter had great control—he could throw any pitch to any spot at any time.

REGGIE JACKSON　　　　　　　　　　　Outfielder

- BORN: 5/18/1946　　• PLAYED FOR TEAM: 1967 TO 1975 & 1987

Reggie Jackson was the most exciting hitter of his time. When he *unleashed* his powerful swing, the ball either jumped off his bat or hissed right past him. Either way, Jackson brought the fans out of their seats.

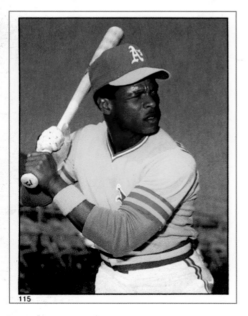

115

RICKEY HENDERSON　　Outfielder

- BORN: 12/25/1958
- PLAYED FOR TEAM: 1979 TO 1984, 1989 TO 1995 & 1998

Rickey Henderson was an amazing **leadoff man**. He was a patient hitter who could draw a walk or smash the ball out of the park. Henderson was also a great base-stealer. In 1982, he set a record with 130 stolen bases. Henderson retired with the most steals (1,406) in baseball history.

ABOVE: Rickey Henderson
RIGHT: Dennis Eckersley

DAVE STEWART — Pitcher

- BORN: 2/19/1957 • PLAYED FOR TEAM: 1986 TO 1992 & 1995

Dave Stewart tried his hand as a **starter** and a **relief pitcher** before joining the A's. After he learned to throw a sinking fastball, he became the only pitcher during the 1980s to win 20 games three seasons in a row.

DENNIS ECKERSLEY — Pitcher

- BORN: 10/3/1954
- PLAYED FOR TEAM: 1987 TO 1995

Dennis Eckersley pitched a **no-hitter** and won 20 games as a young starter. He became a relief pitcher with the A's and led the league in **saves** twice. In 1992, "Eck" won the **Cy Young Award** and was named AL MVP.

DAN HAREN — Pitcher

- BORN: 9/17/1980
- PLAYED FOR TEAM: 2005 TO 2007

After Mark Mulder, Tim Hudson, and Barry Zito spent several years as Oakland's three aces, Dan Haren became the team's top pitcher. He was the starter for the AL in the 2007 **All-Star Game**.

On the Sidelines

In the first half of the 20th century, the story of the A's was the story of Connie Mack. He managed the team from 1901 to 1950 and owned the club for most of that time as well. Mack was known for his intelligence and kindness. He was also a tough businessman. Mack twice sold off his best players to keep the A's afloat. He won nine pennants and five World Series but never spent a day in uniform—he always wore a shirt and tie in the dugout.

During the 1960s and 1970s, Charles Finley owned the A's. Finley was always trying new ideas. Sometimes they worked and sometimes they did not. He often told his players what to do, which made them angry. Finley also argued with his managers. Baseball was never dull when Finley was around!

The A's have had many good managers over the years, including Dick Williams, Alvin Dark, Billy Martin, Tony La Russa, Art Howe, and Ken Macha. Each led the team to the top of the **AL West** at least once during his time in Oakland.

Tony La Russa, who led the A's to three pennants from 1988 to 1990.

One Great Day

The A's were in trouble when the 1972 World Series started. The team, which had not played for the championship in 41 years, was facing the mighty Cincinnati Reds, known throughout baseball as the "Big Red Machine." Oakland's best hitter, Reggie

Jackson, was on crutches. The club's best left-handed reliever, Darold Knowles, had a broken finger. The A's needed a hero. No one guessed that hero would be backup catcher Gene Tenace.

The World Series opened on a chilly October day in Cincinnati. All-Star Gary Nolan took the mound for the Reds in Game One. Many Oakland fans were surprised when manager Dick Williams chose to put Tenace in the starting **lineup**. Dave Duncan was the regular catcher. He had slugged 19 home runs that year. Tenace had hit just five. In the playoffs, however, Tenace showed he might have some magic in his bat. He got the hit that won the pennant for the A's.

Tenace came to bat in the second inning. He promptly knocked a pitch by Nolan out of the park. The Oakland dugout came to life. Three innings later, Tenace hit another home run off of Nolan. He drove in all three runs in Oakland's 3–2 victory. Tenace was the first player in history to slam home runs in his first two World Series **at-bats**.

The A's kept battling the Reds with help from their new star and won the championship four games to three. Tenace scored the winning run in Game Four and in Game Seven. He hit four home runs in all and had nine runs batted in. He was the only Oakland player to drive in more than one run!

LEFT: Gene Tenace, Oakland's unlikely hero in the 1972 World Series.
ABOVE: Tenace stands in the batter's box against the Cincinnati Reds.

Legend Has It

Who was Connie Mack's favorite player?

LEGEND HAS IT that Chief Bender was. The A's had many Hall of Fame players in Mack's 50 years as manager, but Bender was his favorite. Bender tied batters into knots with his great curveball and **changeup**. "If I had all the men I've ever handled and they were in their prime," said Mack, "and there was one game I wanted to win above all others, Chief would be my man."

ABOVE: Chief Bender, Connie Mack's favorite player.

Who was the oldest player to pitch in a big-league game?

LEGEND HAS IT that Satchel Paige was. No one was sure how old Paige was, but he was at least 58 when he took the mound for the A's against the Boston Red Sox in 1965. The team wanted to draw extra fans to the ballpark and hoped they would be excited to watch Paige. He was only supposed to pitch one inning. Instead, Paige pitched three innings—and did not allow a run!

How did a white elephant become the team's mascot?

LEGEND HAS IT that John McGraw was responsible. McGraw was the manager of the New York Giants. During the 1905 season, he was asked what he thought of the A's, since there was a good chance the two teams would meet in the World Series. McGraw called the A's "white elephants," which was a way of saying that they were not as good as they looked. Connie Mack was not *insulted*. In fact, he decided to make the white elephant a *symbol* for the team. Before the first game of the World Series, Mack handed McGraw a toy elephant. They both had a good laugh.

It Really Happened

Back in the early 1900s, when games were often won with bunts and baserunning, a home run was a *remarkable* thing in baseball. Few players tried to hit the ball out of the park, and even fewer were actually able to do it. In 1911, Frank Baker was the AL's home run champion. The Philadelphia star hit a total of 11 long balls.

That season, Baker saved his best for the World Series. The A's faced the New York Giants, a team with many of baseball's toughest pitchers. Fans everywhere expected a thrilling matchup.

In Game Two, Baker came to bat against Rube Marquard in the sixth inning with the score tied 1–1 and a runner on second base. Fans were on the edge of their seats. Marquard threw a ball high and inside, and Baker leaned back and clubbed it. The soaring drive sailed over the fence to give the A's a 3–1 victory.

Game Three was another ***nail-biter***. With the A's trailing 1–0 in the ninth inning, Baker came to bat against Christy Mathewson. The Giants ace threw his famous "fadeaway" pitch, which curved away from Baker. The slugger was ready. He slammed the ball over the fence to tie the game. The A's won in extra innings.

Feeling they could not lose, the A's went on to win the World Series. Their fans celebrated wildly and could not stop talking about the amazing display of power they had ***witnessed***. From that day on, their World Series hero was known as "Home Run" Baker.

"HOME RUN" BAKER

LEFT: Fans line up to buy tickets for the 1911 World Series.
ABOVE: Frank "Home Run" Baker, who earned his nickname with two long balls against the New York Giants.

31

QUIRK
CLUB

Do It RICKEY
←939→
A Bleacher
Bums's
Love You

HENDERSON
24

Team Spirit

In the early days of baseball, team names almost never appeared on uniforms. The players wore the name or initial of their city instead. The A's were the first team to be referred to by its nickname rather than its city name. That was the idea of manager Connie Mack. Since then, the A's have stayed very close to their fans. Even when the club had a poor record or played in an old ballpark, they could still count on cheers of support. In 1981, the "wave" was seen at a **major-league** game for the first time in Oakland.

During the 1960s and 1970s, A's fans cheered for the team's famous mascot, Charlie-O. He was a live mule that belonged to team owner Charles Finley. Charlie-O lived at the ballpark, and Finley often took him to cocktail parties as a joke.

Today, the fans cheer for Stomper, the team's elephant mascot. He arrived in the Oakland Coliseum in 1997, when he rode from center field to home plate on a zip-line. The idea for Stomper came from the white elephant symbol used by the team in the early 1900s.

Rickey Henderson waves to the hometown crowd. The A's have always had a special bond with their fans.

Timeline

Lefty Grove

1910
The A's win their first World Series.

1931
Lefty Grove wins 31 games.

1901
The A's play their first season.

1950
Connie Mack manages the A's for his 50th and final season.

1955
The A's move to Kansas City.

A pennant from the team's early days.

A souvenir from the team's time in Kansas City.

Rickey Henderson

Eric Chavez

1982
Rickey Henderson sets a record with 130 stolen bases.

2002
The A's win 20 games in a row.

2006
Eric Chavez wins his sixth **Gold Glove** in a row.

1968
The A's move to Oakland.

1974
The A's win their third World Series in a row.

1988
Jose Canseco becomes the first player to hit 40 homers and steal 40 bases in the same season.

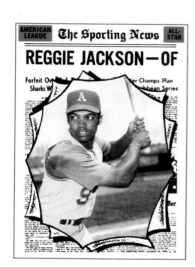

Reggie Jackson, Oakland's top slugger in the 1970s.

Jose Canseco

Fun Facts

TAKING CARE OF BUSINESS

In 2002, Randy Velarde made an **_unassisted_** triple play against the New York Yankees. Earlier that year, in spring training, he also made an unassisted triple play.

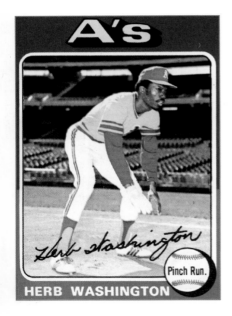

SECOND PLACE

In a 1972 game against the Chicago White Sox, the A's used eight different second basemen.

HERBIE RUNS AGAIN

In 1974, the A's signed track star Herb Washington. He was not a good hitter or fielder, so he was used as the team's **pinch-runner**—it even said so on his baseball card!

FENCE–BUSTER

In 1904, Harry Davis became the first player to win the home run championship four years in a row.

ABOVE: Herb Washington's trading card, which listed him as a pinch-runner.
RIGHT: A team photo shows the members of the 1928 A's.

NEVER COUNT THEM OUT

In Game Four of the 1929 World Series, the A's scored 10 runs in the seventh inning after falling behind 8–0. It was the greatest **comeback** ever in **postseason** play.

SUPERSTARS

In 1928, the A's had seven future Hall of Famers on their team: Ty Cobb, Mickey Cochrane, Jimmie Foxx, Lefty Grove, Eddie Collins, Al Simmons, and Tris Speaker.

TEAM EFFORT

In 1975, Vida Blue, Glenn Abbott, Paul Lindblad, and Rollie Fingers teamed up to no-hit the California Angels.

GOOD DEAL

The A's did not make many good trades during the 1950s, but in 1951 they made a great one. When the season was just four games old, they got Gus Zernial from the Chicago White Sox for a few spare players. Zernial went on to lead the AL in home runs and runs batted in that year!

Talking Baseball

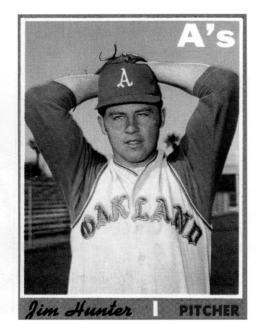

Jim Hunter | PITCHER

"We'd always find a way to beat you …
that's what made the A's so great."
—*Catfish Hunter, on Oakland's championship
teams of the 1970s*

"Sure, I strike out a lot. You don't have a
chance if you don't swing."
—*Reggie Jackson, on the risks of trying
to hit home runs*

"Ever since I was a little kid, the last
thing I wanted to do was lose. I hated losing. I still hate it.
I guess you can see that when I'm out there."
—*Tim Hudson, on the secret to being a winning pitcher*

"I always wanted to be a player, but I never had the talent to make
the big leagues. So I did the next best thing—I bought a team."
—*Charles Finley, on why he became
the owner of the A's*

"When I'm going good, I don't believe there's a batter who can hit me."

> —*Vida Blue, on finding the right rhythm as a pitcher*

"You can't win them all."

> —*Connie Mack, on his 3,776 wins and 4,025 losses*

"When I'm doing well, it's like I'm in a nice little ballet. Everything is going slow all around me. It's very peaceful."

> —*Barry Zito, on staying calm on the pitcher's mound*

"Watch everything and try to avoid making the same mistake twice."

> —*Mickey Cochrane, on improving as a baseball player*

LEFT: Catfish Hunter　　**ABOVE**: Vida Blue

For the Record

The great A's teams and players have left their marks on the record books. These are the "best of the best" ...

Jimmie Foxx

Jason Giambi

A's AWARD WINNERS

WINNER	AWARD	YEAR
Lefty Grove	Most Valuable Player	1931
Jimmie Foxx	Most Valuable Player	1932
Jimmie Foxx	Most Valuable Player	1933
Harry Byrd	Rookie of the Year	1952
Bobby Shantz	Most Valuable Player	1952
Vida Blue	Most Valuable Player	1971
Vida Blue	Cy Young Award	1971
Gene Tenace	World Series MVP	1972
Reggie Jackson	Most Valuable Player	1973
Reggie Jackson	World Series MVP	1973
Catfish Hunter	Cy Young Award	1974
Rollie Fingers	World Series MVP	1974
Jose Canseco	Rookie of the Year	1986
Mark McGwire	Rookie of the Year	1987
Terry Steinbach	All-Star Game MVP	1988
Tony La Russa	Manager of the Year	1988
Walt Weiss	Rookie of the Year	1988
Jose Canseco	Most Valuable Player	1988
Dave Stewart	World Series MVP	1989
Rickey Henderson	Most Valuable Player	1990
Bob Welch	Cy Young Award	1990
Tony La Russa	Manager of the Year	1992
Dennis Eckersley	Most Valuable Player	1992
Dennis Eckersley	Cy Young Award	1992
Ben Grieve	Rookie of the Year	1998
Jason Giambi	Most Valuable Player	2000
Miguel Tejada	Most Valuable Player	2002
Barry Zito	Cy Young Award	2002
Bobby Crosby	Rookie of the Year	2004
Huston Street	Rookie of the Year	2005

A's ACHIEVEMENTS

ACHIEVEMENT	YEAR
AL Pennant Winners	1902
AL Pennant Winners	1905
AL Pennant Winners	1910
World Series Champions	1910
AL Pennant Winners	1911
World Series Champions	1911
AL Pennant Winners	1913
World Series Champions	1913
AL Pennant Winners	1914
AL Pennant Winners	1929
World Series Champions	1929
AL Pennant Winners	1930
World Series Champions	1930
AL Pennant Winners	1931
AL West Champions	1971
AL West Champions	1972
AL Pennant Winners	1972
World Series Champions	1972
AL West Champions	1973
AL Pennant Winners	1973
World Series Champions	1973
AL West Champions	1974
AL Pennant Winners	1974
World Series Champions	1974
AL West Champions	1975
AL West First-Half Champions*	1981
AL West Champions	1988
AL Pennant Winners	1988
AL West Champions	1989
AL Pennant Winners	1989
World Series Champions	1989
AL West Champions	1990
AL Pennant Winners	1990
AL West Champions	1992
AL West Champions	2000
AL West Champions	2002
AL West Champions	2003
AL West Champions	2006

The 1981 season was played with first-half and second-half division winners.

TOP: Huston Street
ABOVE: Mark McGwire

Pinpoints

The history of a baseball team is made up of many smaller stories. These stories take place all over the map—not just in the city a team calls "home." Match the pushpins on these maps to the Team Facts and you will begin to see the story of the A's unfold!

TEAM FACTS

1 Oakland, California—*The A's have played here since 1968.*
2 Pryor, Oklahoma—*Bob Johnson was born here.*
3 Steubenville, Ohio—*Rollie Fingers was born here.*
4 Mansfield, Louisiana—*Vida Blue was born here.*
5 Kansas City, Missouri—*The A's played here from 1955 to 1967.*
6 St. Louis, Missouri—*Ken Holtzman was born here.*
7 Milwaukee, Wisconsin—*Al Simmons was born here.*
8 East Brookfield, Massachusetts—*Connie Mack was born here.*
9 Philadelphia, Pennsylvania—*The A's played here from 1901 to 1954.*
10 Lonaconing, Maryland—*Lefty Grove was born here.*
11 Pueblo Nuevo, Cuba—*Bert Campaneris was born here.*
12 Bani, Dominican Republic—*Miguel Tejada was born here.*

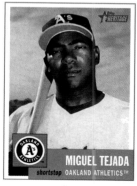

Miguel Tejada

Play Ball

Baseball is a game played between two teams over nine innings. Teams take one turn at bat and one turn in the field during each inning. A turn at bat ends when three outs are made. The batters on the hitting team try to reach base safely. The players on the fielding team try to prevent this from happening.

In baseball, the ball is controlled by the pitcher. The pitcher must throw the ball to the batter, who decides whether or not to swing at each pitch. If a batter swings and misses, it is a strike. If the batter lets a good pitch go by, it is also a strike. If the batter swings and the ball does not stay in fair territory (between the v-shaped lines that begin at home plate) it is called "foul," and is counted as a strike. If the pitcher throws three strikes, the batter is out. If the pitcher throws four bad pitches before that, the batter is awarded first base. This is called a base-on-balls, or "walk."

When the batter swings the bat and hits the ball, everyone springs into action. If a fielder catches a batted ball before it hits the ground, the batter is out. If a fielder scoops the ball off the ground and throws it to first base before the batter arrives, the batter is out. If the batter reaches first base safely, he is credited with a hit. A one-base hit is called a single, a two-base hit is called a double, a three-base hit is called a triple, and a four-base hit is called a home run.

Runners who reach base are only safe when they are touching one of the bases. If they are caught between the bases, the fielders can tag them with the ball and record an out.

A batter who is able to circle the bases and make it back to home plate before three outs are made is credited with a run scored. The team with the most runs after nine innings is the winner.

Anyone who has played baseball (or softball) knows that it can be a complicated game. Every player on the field has a job to do. Different players have different strengths and weaknesses. The pitchers, batters, and managers make hundreds of decisions every game. The more you play and watch baseball, the more "little things" you are likely to notice. The next time you are at a game, look for these plays:

PLAY LIST

DOUBLE PLAY—A play where the fielding team is able to make two outs on one batted ball. This usually happens when a runner is on first base, and the batter hits a ground ball to one of the infielders. The base runner is forced out at second base and the ball is then thrown to first base before the batter arrives.

HIT AND RUN—A play where the runner on first base sprints to second base while the pitcher is throwing the ball to the batter. When the second baseman or shortstop moves toward the base to wait for the catcher's throw, the batter tries to hit the ball to the place that the fielder has just left. If the batter swings and misses, the fielding team can tag the runner out.

INTENTIONAL WALK—A play when the pitcher throws four bad pitches on purpose, allowing the batter to walk to first base. This happens when the pitcher would much rather face the next batter—and is willing to risk putting a runner on base.

SACRIFICE BUNT—A play where the batter makes an out on purpose so that a teammate can move to the next base. On a bunt, the batter tries to "deaden" the pitch with the bat instead of swinging at it.

SHOESTRING CATCH—A play where an outfielder catches a short hit an inch or two above the ground, near the tops of his shoes. It is not easy to run as fast as you can and lower your glove without slowing down. It can be risky, too. If a fielder misses a shoestring catch, the ball might roll all the way to the fence.

45

Glossary

BASEBALL WORDS TO KNOW

AL WEST—A group of American League teams that plays in the western part of the country.

ALL-STAR GAME—Baseball's annual game featuring the best players from the American League and National League.

AMERICAN LEAGUE (AL)—One of baseball's two major leagues; the AL began play in 1901 and the National League (NL) started in 1876.

AT-BATS—Turns hitting. "At-bats" are also a statistic that helps to measure how many times a player comes to the plate.

CHANGEUP—A slow pitch disguised to look like a fastball.

CY YOUNG AWARD—The annual trophy given to each league's best pitcher.

EARNED RUN AVERAGE (ERA)—A statistic that counts how many runs a pitcher gives up for every nine innings he pitches.

FEDERAL LEAGUE—A third major league that played two seasons, 1914 and 1915.

GOLD GLOVE—An award given each year to baseball's best fielders.

HALL OF FAME—The museum in Cooperstown, New York, where baseball's greatest players are honored. A player voted into the Hall of Fame is sometimes called a "Hall of Famer."

LEADOFF MAN—The first hitter in a lineup, or the first hitter in an inning.

LINEUP—The list of players who are playing in a game.

MAJOR-LEAGUE—Belonging to the American League or National League, which make up the major leagues.

MOST VALUABLE PLAYER (MVP)—An award given each year to each league's top player; an MVP is also selected for the World Series and All-Star Game.

NO-HITTER—A game in which a team is unable to get a hit.

PENNANT—A league championship. The term comes from the triangular flag awarded to each season's champion, beginning in the 1870s.

PINCH-RUNNER—A player who is sent into the game to run for a teammate.

PITCHING STAFF—The group of players who pitch for a team.

PLAYOFFS—The games played after the regular season to determine which teams will advance to the World Series.

POSTSEASON—The games played after the regular season, including the playoffs and World Series.

RELIEF PITCHER—A pitcher who is brought into a game to replace another pitcher. Relief pitchers can be seen warming up in the bullpen.

ROOKIE OF THE YEAR—The annual award given to each league's best first-year player.

RUNS BATTED IN (RBI)—A statistic that counts the number of runners a batter drives home.

SAVES—A statistic that counts the number of times a relief pitcher finishes off a close victory for his team.

SLUGGERS—Powerful hitters.

STARTER—The pitcher who begins the game for his team.

TRIPLE CROWN—An honor given to a player who leads the league in home runs, batting average, and runs batted in.

WORLD SERIES—The world championship series played between the winners of the National League and American League.

OTHER WORDS TO KNOW

CENTURY—A period of 100 years.

COMEBACK—The process of catching up from behind, or making up a large deficit.

DIVERSE—Having many different groups.

DRAMATIC—Exciting or historic.

DYNAMIC—Exciting and energetic.

EVAPORATE—Disappear, or turn into vapor.

FLANNEL—A soft wool or cotton material.

INSULTED—Spoke to someone in a way that hurts their feelings.

LOGO—A symbol or design that represents a company or team.

MASCOT—An animal or person believed to bring a group good luck.

NAIL-BITER—A close, tense game.

PATIENT—Able to wait calmly.

REMARKABLE—Unusual or exceptional.

STRATEGIES—Plans or methods for succeeding.

SYMBOL—Something that represents a thought or idea.

SYNTHETIC—Made in a laboratory, not in nature.

WITNESSED—Saw something happen in person.

UNASSISTED—Without help from anyone.

UNLEASHED—Let loose.

Places to Go

ON THE ROAD

OAKLAND A'S
7000 Coliseum Way
Oakland, California 94621
(510) 638-4900

NATIONAL BASEBALL HALL OF FAME AND MUSEUM
25 Main Street
Cooperstown, New York 13326
(888) 425-5633
www.baseballhalloffame.org

ON THE WEB

THE OAKLAND A'S
- *Learn more about the A's*

www.oaklandathletics.com

MAJOR LEAGUE BASEBALL
- *Learn more about all the major league teams*

www.mlb.com

MINOR LEAGUE BASEBALL
- *Learn more about the minor leagues*

www.minorleaguebaseball.com

ON THE BOOKSHELF

To learn more about the sport of baseball, look for these books at your library or bookstore:

- Kelly, James. *Baseball*. New York, New York: DK, 2005.
- Jacobs, Greg. *The Everything Kids' Baseball Book*. Cincinnati, Ohio: Adams Media Corporation, 2006.
- Stewart, Mark and Kennedy, Mike. *Long Ball: The Legend and Lore of the Home Run*. Minneapolis, Minnesota: Millbrook Press, 2006.

Index

PAGE NUMBERS IN **BOLD** REFER TO ILLUSTRATIONS.

The Team

MARK STEWART has written more than 25 books on baseball, and over 100 sports books for kids. He grew up in New York City during the 1960s rooting for the Yankees and Mets, and now takes his two daughters, Mariah and Rachel, to the same ballparks. Mark comes from a family of writers. His grandfather was Sunday Editor of the *New York Times* and his mother was Articles Editor of *Ladies' Home Journal* and *McCall's*. Mark has profiled hundreds of athletes over the last 20 years. He has also written several books about his native New York and New Jersey, his home today. Mark is a graduate of Duke University, with a degree in history. He lives with his daughters and wife, Sarah, overlooking Sandy Hook, NJ.

JAMES L. GATES, JR. has served as Library Director at the National Baseball Hall of Fame since 1995. He had previously served in academic libraries for almost fifteen years. He holds degrees from Belmont Abbey College, the University of Notre Dame, and Indiana University. During his career Jim has authored several academic articles and has served in an editorial capacity on multiple book, magazine, and museum publications, and he also serves as host for the Annual Cooperstown Symposium on Baseball and American Culture. He is an ardent Baltimore Orioles fan and enjoys watching baseball with his wife and two children.